Ballerina Gets Ready

by Allegra Kent

illustrated by
Catherine Stock

Holiday House / New York

I<small>RIS</small> wakes up. It is **8:00** in the morning. At 8:00 tonight, she will be dancing in one of her favorite ballets.

8:30. After a quick hot shower, she gets dressed and has tea, eggs—scrambled today—and toast with a bit of butter.

At **9:00** Iris packs her practice bag: pointe shoes, water, snacks, phone, a good book and a sandwich.

9:15. She's on her way. Iris walks past buildings, trees, dogs, buses, cars, many people and many, many pigeons. Up they go!

At **10:00** Iris enters the theater through the stage door that dancers, musicians, stagehands, lighting crew, wardrobe mistresses, the ballet master—all who work on the performance—use.

"Hello, Henry!" she says to the guard.

10:05. In her dressing room, Iris puts on practice clothes: leotard, tights, sweater, shorts and an old pair of shoes.

Her roommate, Violet, comes in at **10:15**.

"How is your day?" Violet asks.

"Packed," says Iris. "Class, rehearsals, fittings . . . and I'm working with Alexi on the new ballet."

Iris goes to the practice room, where other dancers are gathering.

The ballet master arrives to give the company class. They start with the *barre*.

"Point those toes!" the ballet master says.

At **11:00** the class moves to the center of the floor, where they do an *adagio*.

11:30. When class is over, Iris returns to her dressing room for a wipe down and a banana. Violet is sewing the ribbons on her shoes.

At 12:00 Iris is back in the practice room. The choreographer, Alexi, is making a new ballet; and Iris and her partner, Michael, are going to be in it!

"Let's start with the first pose," Alexi says. "No, no. This is not working."

At **12:01** Alexi says, "This is good! Really good!"

At **1:30** rehearsal ends.

"Excellent! Thank you, Iris. Thank you, Michael."

Now Iris has some free time.
At **2:00** she is back home,
where she waters her plants,
cuddles her cat and rests with her
book.

At 2:30 . . .

"Oh, my!" Iris says.
"It's **3:00** already!"

At **3:30** Iris is back at the
theater. In the costume shop, she tries
on a long tutu for the new ballet.

"A little tighter here," she says.

"A little longer would be good," the
designer says.

At **4:00** Alexi calls everyone onstage to rehearse tonight's
performance.

Michael jumps into a breathtaking double *tour en l'air* . . .
but twists his foot as he lands.

"Will you be able to dance tonight?" Alexi asks.

"I'm afraid not," Michael says.

Iris will dance with
Billy instead. Iris and
Billy have never danced
together, so they practice
for the rest of the
afternoon.

At **6:00** Iris takes a break for a small dinner.

And at **6:30** she's back
in her dressing room to apply
her makeup, arrange her hair
and choose her shoes. "Too
hard . . . too soft . . . just
right." She puts them aside
for later.

At **7:00** Iris is in the wings of the stage, where she does a short *barre* with Billy and the other dancers.

At **7:20** Iris is back in her dressing room, where she puts on her tights and her pointe shoes. The dresser comes in to fasten Iris's costume.

"Half hour to curtain," the stage manager announces over the loudspeaker. It's time for the dancers to make their way backstage.

Iris puts the tips of her pointe shoes into the rosin box. She checks her ribbons—not too tight, not too loose—and tucks in the ends.

Onstage, dancers jog, stretch and chat.

"Ten minutes to curtain," the stage manager calls.

On the other side of the curtain,
the musicians are warming up.

Iris stands with her back straight, her shoulders down, her neck stretched and her head high. She thinks about dancing as well as she can—for the audience, for the choreographer and for herself. Billy smiles at her, and she smiles back.

It's **8:00**. The lights go down, and a hush settles over the house.
The audience applauds when the conductor reaches the podium.
Music fills the theater, and the curtain rises.

The magic begins.

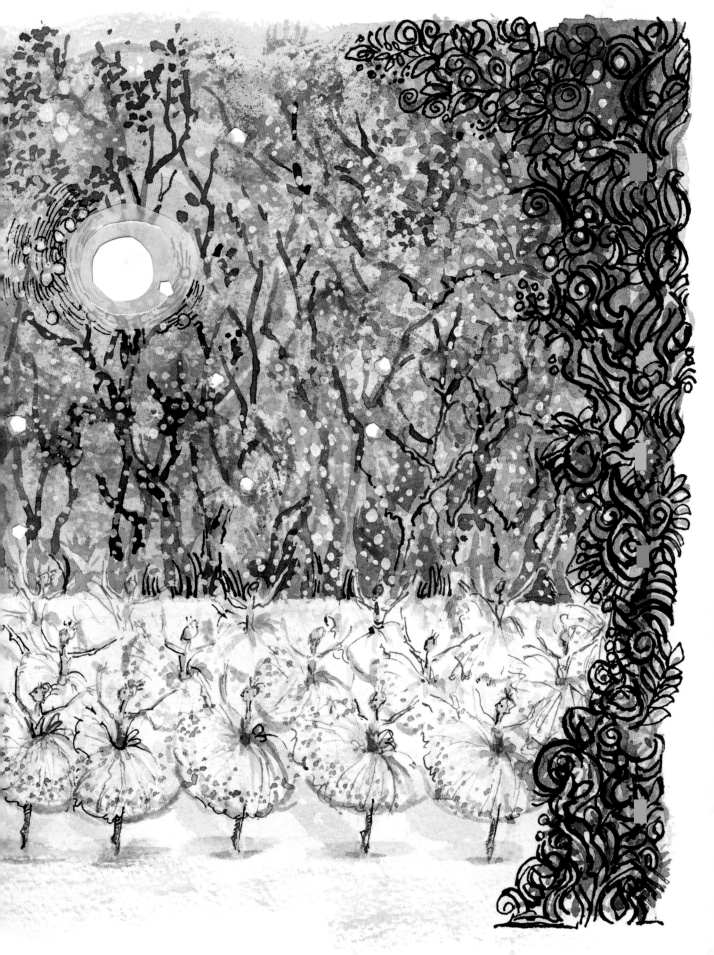

Text copyright © 2016 by Allegra Kent
Illustrations copyright © 2016 by Catherine Stock
All Rights Reserved
HOLIDAY HOUSE is registered in the U.S. Patent and Trademark Office.
Printed and Bound in November 2015 at Toppan Leefung, DongGuan City, China.
The artwork was created with pen and ink and watercolors.
www.holidayhouse.com
First Edition
1 3 5 7 9 10 8 6 4 2

Library of Congress Cataloging-in-Publication Data
Kent, Allegra.
Ballerina gets ready / by Allegra Kent ; illustrated by Catherine Stock. — First edition.
pages cm
Summary: "From the time she wakes at 8 a.m. until the curtain rises at 8 p.m., a prima ballerina's day is busy,
busy, busy with classes, rehearsals and fittings, as well as meals and friendship"— Provided by publisher.
ISBN 978-0-8234-3563-0 (hardcover)
[1. Ballet--Fiction.] I. Stock, Catherine, illustrator. II. Title.
PZ7.K4123Bai 2016
[E]—dc23
2015022329